The Berenstain Bears
and the

DRESS CODE

by Stan & Jan Berenstain

A BIG CHAPTER BOOK™

Random House 🏠 New York

All rights reserved under International and Pan-American Copyright
Conventions. Published in the United States by Random House, Inc.,
New York, and simultaneously in Canada by Random House of
Canada Limited, Toronto.

Library of Congress Cataloging-in-Publication Data
Berenstain, Stan.
The Berenstain Bears and the dress code /
by Stan and Jan Berenstain.
 p. cm. — (A big chapter book)
SUMMARY: Even though they are not into rad fashions, Brother Bear
and Sister Bear join the other cubs' protest when Mr. Grizzmeyer
enforces a strict dress code at Bear Country School.
ISBN 0-679-86665-5 (pbk.) — ISBN 0-679-96665-X (lib. bdg.)
[1. Clothing and dress—Fiction.   2. Schools—Fiction.
3. Bears—Fiction.] I. Berenstain, Jan.   II. Title.
III. Series: Berenstain, Stan.   Big chapter book.
PZ7.B4483Bede   1994
[Fic]—dc20   94-19826

Manufactured in the United States of America 10 9 8

BIG CHAPTER BOOKS is a trademark of Berenstain Enterprises, Inc.

Contents

Chapter 1
Spring Fashions

Spring was the time of year for new things in Bear Country. Not just new leaves and flowers, but new fads and fashions, too. It seemed that every spring the cubs at Bear Country School wore clothes that were a different style from last spring's clothes. Skirts were usually a little shorter or longer. Blue jeans were a little tighter or looser.

The teachers and other grownups who worked at Bear Country School never paid much attention to these changing cub fashions.

But one spring, cub fashions didn't change a little. They changed *a lot*.

It all started with boys wearing their baseball caps backward at recess. Soon jeans got more and more faded, and more and more worn at the knees. Until they wore right through!

"Whoa!" Sister Bear said to Lizzy Bruin one morning. "Aren't those kneeholes kind of big?"

Lizzy and Sister stood with a crowd of cubs at the schoolyard waiting for the morning bell to ring. Around them were all sorts of unusual clothes. Barry Bruin had on a jacket with a picture of The Monster That Ate Big Bear City printed on the back. Babs

Bruno was wearing two anklets on each ankle and a ring on each toe. The Too-Tall gang members wore sweatshirts with messages on them. Skuzz's said GET LOST.

Smirk's had BUZZ OFF printed on it. And Vinnie's said DROP DEAD. Too-Tall himself wore a long black Batbear cape.

Lizzy looked down at her gaping knee-holes. "Way cool, aren't they?" she said to Sister. "By the way, when are you going to join us 'rads' in the 'kneehole look'?"

The cubs who wore the new fashions called themselves "rads," from the word "radical," meaning extreme or different. Sister didn't feel extreme or different. She just felt like herself. But she did like the "kneehole look."

Papa would hit the roof

"They do look kind of cool," she said. "But I'm not really into rad clothes. Besides, Papa would hit the roof if he saw me in those."

"Drop by my house on the way to school tomorrow and borrow a pair of mine," said Lizzy. "Then change back into your regular clothes on the way home. What Papa doesn't know won't hurt him—or you."

"Thanks, anyway," said Sister, "but I'll stick with my regular outfit for now. Aren't you worried you'll get a warning from Teacher Jane about those kneeholes?"

"So what if I do?" said Lizzy. "I've got jeans with all different-size kneeholes at home. Besides, Teacher Jane says we're allowed to have kneeholes as long as they aren't too big. How will we find out what's 'too big' if we don't experiment?"

"I guess you're right," said Sister. "All I

can say is, you're lucky you're not in Miss Glitch's class. She won't even allow jeans that are a little worn in the knees."

Figuring out what their teachers would think of new clothing styles was a problem for the cubs. Some teachers, like Teacher Jane and Teacher Bob, were pretty easygoing about the rad clothes. But others, like Miss Glitch, hated them. The toughest of all was Mr. Grizzmeyer, the vice principal and gym teacher. Usually he left the decisions about clothes up to the classroom teachers. But when Vinnie of the Too-Tall gang came to school one day with a spiky punk hair style, Mr. Grizzmeyer told him that he would be suspended for *the rest of the year* if he ever tried it again.

"I'm even luckier that we wear uniforms for gym," laughed Lizzy. "Can you imagine what it would be like if Mr. Grizzmeyer

were in charge of making the rules about clothes? He might even ban your hair ribbon!"

Sister might have laughed, too, if she'd been listening. But she was deep in thought. "It isn't fair," she said finally with a frown.

"What isn't fair?" asked Lizzy.

"That Teacher Jane's cubs are allowed to wear rad clothes and Miss Glitch's cubs aren't. We're even in the same grade!"

"Life isn't fair," said Lizzy. It didn't bother her a bit that Miss Glitch's cubs weren't allowed to wear rad clothes. Just as long as *she* got to wear them.

"Well, I think it's pretty darn confusing," said Sister. "Somebody ought to do something about it."

"Don't hold your breath," said Lizzy. "Things will have to get pretty stirred up around here first."

Just then Sister spied Queenie McBear coming down the street. "Funny you should say that," she said.

"Why?" asked Lizzy.

Sister pointed at Queenie. "Here comes somebody who just might do the stirring up."

Queenie had on an outfit that was like nothing the cubs had ever seen at Bear Country School. A bright red body stocking with a very, very, *very* short miniskirt.

Chapter 2
The Miniskirt and Miss Glitch

There were whistles from the Too-Tall gang as Queenie came into the schoolyard. All the cubs turned to look. Too-Tall yelled, "Hey, guys, get a load of Miss Miniskirt. *Woo-woo!*"

The on-again, off-again thing between Queenie and Too-Tall was off again that week. So Queenie walked right past Too-Tall and joined some of her friends from Teacher Bob's class.

"Well, guys, what do you think?" she asked.

No one spoke for a moment. Even though Brother Bear and Cousin Fred didn't really like the rad clothes, they weren't against them, either. But Queenie's outfit left them speechless.

Finally, Babs Bruno said, "Way cool!"

"Awesome!" said Trudy Brunowitz.

Trudy, Ferdy Factual's girlfriend, had been wearing jeans with kneeholes for a few weeks now. She had even started speaking the rads' slang. But Ferdy was still in his nerdy cap, vest, and knickers.

Ferdy gave Trudy a bored look and said, "I'm not sure awe is the true emotion inspired by Queenie's new outfit."

"No?" said Queenie. "Then what is?"

Ferdy didn't answer.

"Well?" said Queenie.

"Don't rush me," said Ferdy. "I'm trying to decide between 'disgust' and 'amusement.'"

"Very funny," said Queenie. "Hey, Trudy, your nerdy boyfriend is a pain in the neck."

"He *is* getting to be kind of a bore," grumbled Trudy.

"*Getting* to be?" said Ferdy. "I'm the same bore I've always been! *You're* the one who has changed!"

I'M TRYING TO DECIDE BETWEEN "DISGUST" AND "AMUSEMENT."

"Chill out, Ferd," said Trudy. "We'll discuss it later in private—if you're lucky." She turned to Queenie. "*I* think it's a really cool outfit, Queenie. But what will Teacher Bob say?"

"Oh, Teacher Bob's a sweetheart," said Queenie. "From the moment I walk into class this morning until the time I walk out this afternoon, Teacher Bob won't say a word."

Queenie might have been right about Teacher Bob. But no one had a chance to find out. Because Queenie never even got to Teacher Bob's class.

After the bell rang, Queenie was stopped in the hall by the teacher on hall duty. Unfortunately for Queenie, the teacher on hall duty that morning was Miss Glitch. The other cubs stood to one side and waited for Miss Glitch to finish with Queenie.

Miss Glitch put her hands on her hips and looked down her nose at Queenie. "And just where do you think *you're* going?" she asked.

"To class," said Queenie.

Miss Glitch looked Queenie up and down. "Dressed like *that*?"

"I'm pretty sure it'll be okay with Teacher Bob," said Queenie.

"You may be right," said Miss Glitch. "But it's *not* okay with *me*. You show a complete lack of respect for your school, the teachers, and your fellow students when you wear such clothing to school. How can you expect your classmates to learn anything with you dressed like that? Go home and change this very minute!"

Queenie looked surprised. And hurt, too. "But...but...," she stammered. "But you're not even my teacher."

"No," said Miss Glitch. "But I *am* the teacher on hall duty. Therefore, I have the right to handle any problems that arise in the halls this morning. And in my opinion, *you* are this morning's biggest problem."

Queenie looked at her friends. Her eyes filled with tears. Then she turned and ran down the hall and out the front door.

Miss Glitch looked over at the other cubs. "Well, what are you all staring at?" she snapped. "Hurry up or you'll be late for class!"

Chapter 3
A Growing Problem

Not long after Miss Glitch sent Queenie home from school, Mr. Honeycomb, the school principal, was sitting at his desk going over the week's schedule one last time. He had come in before the start of the school day that morning because he was planning to leave early—in just a few minutes, in fact.

Mr. Honeycomb was about to drive to Big Bear City for a special principals' meeting at Bear Country University. He was looking forward to it. Even though the meeting would last for three full days, he wasn't worried about Bear Country School being without a principal. Mr. Grizzmeyer would take care of everything.

Mr. Honeycomb closed his schedule book and reached for his suit jacket. Just then the telephone rang.

"Oh, hello, Ms. McBear," said Mr. Honeycomb. "How are you?"

"Very upset," said the voice at the other end. "Just like my daughter."

"What's the trouble?" asked Mr. Honeycomb.

"Don't you think a hall-duty teacher should check with a cub's regular teacher before sending her home from school?"

"Yes, I certainly do," said Mr. Honeycomb. "Why do you ask?"

"You don't know?" said Ms. McBear. "Miss Glitch didn't even check with *you* before sending Queenie home?"

"Oh, dear," said Mr. Honeycomb. "I'm afraid not. Why was Queenie sent home?"

Ms. McBear described Queenie's new outfit.

"My, that *is* a new outfit," said Mr. Honeycomb. "Where in the world did she get the idea for that?"

"From an old snapshot of me as a cub wearing exactly the same thing," said

Queenie's mother. "Do you really think it's a good idea to send a cub home, without even a warning, for wearing something her mother once wore?"

"Well,…I…er…maybe not," said Mr. Honeycomb. "But I certainly agree that I should have been told about this. I really have to go, Ms. McBear. But I promise I'll look into this matter. Good-bye."

Mr. Honeycomb placed his elbows on the desk and put his head between his hands. Until now, he hadn't been too worried about the rads and their unusual clothes. He felt that if the rads were allowed to wear their clothes, everything would be okay. What had him worried were the teachers and their different sets of rules. And now Miss Glitch had gone way too far—just when he had to go out of town for three days!

Mr. Honeycomb switched on his intercom and asked Mr. Grizzmeyer to come in. A moment later, the vice principal appeared at the door. "What's up, chief?" he asked.

Mr. Honeycomb told Mr. Grizzmeyer what had happened.

"Well, I don't agree with the way Miss Glitch went about it," said Mr. Grizzmeyer, "but at least her heart's in the right place."

The principal sighed. "You know how I feel, Mr. G.," he said. "I don't much care what style clothes the cubs wear to school, as long as their bodies are more or less covered."

"That's the problem!" said Mr. Grizzmeyer. "They should be *more* covered, not *less!*"

Mr. Honeycomb already had his jacket on. "I've got to go," he said, grabbing his briefcase. "While I'm away, I don't want anyone sent home unless he or she is wearing something so unusual that it will keep the other students from paying attention in class. If we make a big deal out of these rad clothes, the cubs will just keep trying stranger and stranger ones. Please talk to Miss Glitch for me. And keep an eye on her."

"You bet, Mr. H.," said Mr. Grizzmeyer.

"Don't worry about a thing."

Don't worry about a thing? thought Mr. Honeycomb as he hurried through the parking lot to his car. Had he really asked Mr. Grizzmeyer to keep an eye on Miss Glitch? Wasn't that a bit like asking a wolf to keep an eye on the fox that's been prowling around the chicken coop?

YOU BET, MR. H. DON'T WORRY ABOUT A THING.

Chapter 4
A Family Discussion

Later that afternoon, discussions were going on in living rooms all over Bear Country. The news about Queenie and Miss Glitch had spread quickly. It had brought the school dress problem out into the open.

The discussion at the Bear family's tree house was typical. Miss Glitch had support, but so did Queenie.

As usual, Papa was the first to give his opinion. "No cub has any business wearing a short, short miniskirt to school," he said firmly. "I say Queenie got what she deserved."

"Without even a warning?" said Sister. "Just for wearing something her mom wore as a cub?"

"If Ms. McBear had worn that to school," said Papa, "*she* would have been sent home, too!"

"But it isn't fair," said Sister. "Miss Glitch isn't Queenie's teacher. Teacher Bob would have let her into class."

"I'm all in favor of fairness," said Papa. "I don't think *any* cub should be allowed to wear a miniskirt or torn jeans to school."

Sister rolled her eyes. "Oh, great!" she said. "Maybe we should just all wear uniforms to school!"

"Not a bad idea," said Papa. "I'll bring it up at the next PTA meeting!"

"Now hold on," said Mama. "Let's try to discuss this without getting angry at one another."

"I'm not angry!" growled Papa.

"Me neither!" snarled Sister.

"Of course not," said Mama. "That's why I'm sure you'll agree that it's very confusing to have different rules for different classes. We all want fairness. The question is, how much freedom should there be for cubs to

wear whatever they want? I don't have a problem with cubs wearing what they want, unless it's so weird that no one can pay attention in class. And as long as they aren't half-naked."

"Or *completely* naked," added Papa.

"That goes without saying," said Sister, rolling her eyes again.

"Nowadays I'm not sure there's *anything* that goes without saying," grumbled Papa. He looked over at Brother. "You haven't said a word, Brother," said Papa. "I hope you're not in favor of all this dress-freedom stuff, too."

Brother shrugged. "Yes and no," he said. "I'm not into rad clothes myself. But it doesn't bother me when other cubs wear them to school."

Papa sighed. "I guess that's the important thing," he said. "I don't mind if you cubs are in favor of dress freedom. Just so you don't *do* it."

That was no problem for Brother. He had never even thought of trying any of the rad clothes. In fact, he didn't much care about clothing styles at all.

But Sister felt differently. She was already angry about what Miss Glitch had done to Queenie. And when she heard Papa say, "Just so you don't *do* it," she got even angrier. It really bothered her when her parents told her not to do something that all her friends were doing. And in the back of her mind, she had been thinking about trying out the kneehole look.

Suddenly, Sister remembered Lizzy's suggestion. I'll show them! she thought. Tomorrow morning I'll stop at Lizzy's and borrow a pair of jeans with kneeholes big enough for *basketballs* to fit through!

Chapter 5
Dress Wars

As it turned out, Sister Bear wasn't the only cub who was angry about what Miss Glitch had done to Queenie or about what her parents had to say about it. The next morning, dozens of cubs who had never worn rad clothes to school showed up in cutoffs and jeans with kneeholes.

Some cubs who had been wearing rad clothes all along came to school in rad clothes that were even more far-out. Babs Bruno wore *three* anklets on each ankle and *two* rings on each toe. To his monster jacket, Barry Bruin added a pair of jeans with one long leg and one cutoff leg. And Trudy Brunowitz showed up in a pair of paint-spattered jeans that looked a lot like the overalls worn by Grizzly Gus, the school custodian, when he was painting.

The cubs couldn't help noticing that Ferdy Factual wasn't with Trudy. It looked as if the two weren't even speaking to each other. *The dress wars were on!*

And Mr. Grizzmeyer was ready for them. As the cubs came into school, he patrolled the halls himself, with a whistle in his mouth and a stern look on his face. The whistle squealed again and again as he

stopped cubs and warned them about their clothing.

The next day, even more cubs showed up in rad clothes. This time Mr. Grizzmeyer made Miss Glitch his deputy hall patrol. But even with two grownups on hall patrol, there were so many rad clothes that the patrol could give warnings only for the weirdest of them.

Too-Tall and his gang were sent home that day. They had come to school wearing T-shirts with SCHOOL STINKS painted on them.

Mr. Grizzmeyer was afraid they might come back wearing something even worse. But they didn't. In fact, they didn't come back at all that day. Instead, they went fishing out at Bear Creek and planned what to wear to school the next day.

Chapter 6
Too-Tall's Surprise

By the third and final day of Mr. Honeycomb's principals' meeting, the rad fashions at Bear Country School had really taken off. Sister Bear was beginning to feel left behind in her borrowed jeans with kneeholes. Lizzy Bruin's kneeholes sagged almost to her ankles, and Barry Bruin's cut-offs had climbed to the tops of his thighs. Babs Bruno had added so many toe rings and anklets that she clicked and jangled when she walked. And Trudy Brunowitz's paint-spattered jeans seemed to be all paint and no jeans.

But the most shocking fashion statements that day were made by Queenie McBear

and Too-Tall Grizzly. Their on-again, off-again thing was on again. They arrived at school arm in arm.

"Oh, my gosh," gasped Lizzy Bruin when she saw Queenie and Too-Tall coming down the street. "Look at Queenie! She finally figured out how to get away with wearing that miniskirt!"

Sister's eyebrows raised as she looked. "Get away with it?" she said. "Don't be so sure."

Queenie was indeed wearing her short, short miniskirt again. But she was wearing it over a pair of jeans. Well, sort of jeans. It was hard to tell if they were jeans or a bunch of patched-together old rags. They were full of holes. They had so many holes, in fact, that they looked more like a pair of holes with jeans in them than a pair of jeans with holes in them.

Queenie and Too-Tall went up to a group of admiring classmates. With one hand on her hip and the other behind her head, Queenie said, "Well, what do you think of me *now*?"

"Totally awesome!" said Babs Bruno.

"Way way WAY cool!" said Trudy Brunowitz.

"But what about you, Too-Tall?" asked Barry Bruin.

"Whadd'ya mean?" said Too-Tall.

"He means," said Cousin Fred, "how can you stand showing up in that same old Bat-bear cape when your girlfriend has just broken the fashion meter? I'm not even sure we can call that cape 'rad' anymore."

Too-Tall smiled. "You want rad?" he said. "I'll give you rad." He turned his head so that something on his ear caught the morning sun.

The other cubs gasped. It was an earring! Not a big one or a fancy one. Just a small round gold one. But it was still an earring. No boy cub had ever worn an earring to school before.

"Outta sight!" said Babs. Then she called out, "Hey, everybody! Too-Tall's wearing an earring!"

All the cubs in the schoolyard crowded around to see Too-Tall's gold earring glinting in the sunlight. "Ooh" and "aah" they all said at once.

"Glad you like it," said Too-Tall, looking around at the cubs. He motioned for them to crowd in even closer. In a whisper loud enough for all to hear, he said, "Just between you and me, I'm only wearing it to get Mr. Grizzmeyer to blow his top. It'll be fun to see him make a fool of himself."

Too-Tall turned to Ferdy Factual. "What

do you think my chances are, Mr. Genius?"

Ferdy put a finger to his mouth and thought for a moment. "Ninety-nine point ninety-nine percent," he said.

"What's that mean in English?" asked Too-Tall.

"It means it's a cinch," said Ferdy. "By the way, did you have your ear pierced?"

"Sure," said Too-Tall. "Sure I did."

"Let's see! Let's see!" squealed Babs, jumping up and down.

"Are you callin' me a liar?" snarled Too-Tall.

"Uh, no," said Babs quickly. "No way, big guy."

"That's better," said Too-Tall. He gave Ferdy a suspicious look. "Why did you ask that?" he said.

"Simple," said Ferdy. "It changes my calculations of the probability of your making

Mr. G. blow his top. It's a *double* cinch now. A hundred percent sure."

Queenie put an arm around Too-Tall's waist and grinned. "This is our secret plan to get rid of Mr. Grizzmeyer until Mr. Honeycomb gets back tomorrow," she said.

"Get rid of Mr. G.?" said Brother Bear. "How do you figure that?"

"Because the instant Mr. G. sees me and Too-Tall," said Queenie, "he'll go so far through the roof it'll take him until tomorrow to come down."

Chapter 7
A Mild Response

The morning school bell rang. The cubs marched through the front door and down the main hallway. Queenie and Too-Tall led the way.

"Just a minute, you two," said a gruff voice as they passed the principal's office. Out came Mr. Grizzmeyer. He stood in front of Queenie and Too-Tall with his arms folded across his chest.

"Where's his whistle?" Cousin Fred whispered to Brother Bear.

"He hasn't got it," Brother whispered back. "And where's Miss Glitch? She's supposed to be his deputy."

Too-Tall grinned up at Mr. Grizzmeyer and said, "How's it goin', Mr. G.? Like my new earring?" He turned his head to show it off.

"And he even got his ear pierced!" said Queenie.

The cubs got ready for the biggest explosion of yelling that had ever been heard in the halls of Bear Country School. But nothing happened. In fact, Mr. Grizzmeyer was smiling.

"Well?" said Too-Tall. "You hate it, don't you?"

Mr. Grizzmeyer just kept smiling.

"I'm a guy, remember?" said Too-Tall. He sounded puzzled. "You hate to see a guy wearing something a girl might wear. Right?"

"You're right," said Mr. Grizzmeyer with a chuckle. "I think your earring looks absolutely ridiculous."

"Then go ahead and send me home," said Too-Tall. "Suspend me if you want—see if I care."

"Send you home? Suspend you?" said Mr. Grizzmeyer. "Not today, Too-Tall."

Queenie was as confused as the rest of the cubs. "What about me, Mr. Grizzmeyer?" she asked. "Look at my jeans!"

"Jeans?" said Mr. Grizzmeyer. "I thought maybe you were playing at the garbage dump and some old greasy rags got stuck to your legs."

Everyone laughed.

"Then you're mad, right?" said Queenie.

"I'm very busy today," said Mr. Grizzmeyer, heading back to the office. "I've got a lot of work to do."

"You mean you're not going to get mad?" said Queenie. "You're going to let us wear these super-rad things?"

"Yes," said Mr. Grizzmeyer calmly. "Enjoy them while you can."

And with that, Mr. Grizzmeyer went into the office and closed the door. The cubs were left staring at one another with their mouths wide open.

"What's going on?" said Barry Bruin.

"Has Mr. G. flipped?" asked Babs Bruno.

"And what did he mean by 'Enjoy them while you can'?" asked Cousin Fred.

"Perhaps," said Ferdy Factual, "he's going to call Queenie's mom and Too-Tall's dad and make them take the cubs home."

"I'll bet Ferdy's right," said Barry. "Boy, what a scene *that'll* be! Two-Ton Grizzly dragging Too-Tall out of class by the ear!"

The cubs hurried to class.

All day they waited for Two-Ton to come roaring in. But he never showed up.

As for Mr. Grizzmeyer, he was not seen again that day in either the classrooms or the hallway.

Chapter 8
Bad News and Worse News

Later that afternoon, Brother and Sister Bear and their friends were having milk shakes in their favorite booth at the Burger Bear. Trudy Brunowitz and Ferdy Factual were both there. But they were sitting across from each other, not together. It seemed they just couldn't stop arguing in front of their friends.

"My paint-spattered jeans are just too rad

for Ferdy," Trudy told Babs Bruno.

"Nonsense," said Ferdy. "Being 'rad' is being different from everyone else. Nearly all the cubs are wearing weird jeans now. You're just a conformist."

All the cubs except Trudy and Ferdy turned to Cousin Fred, who liked to read the dictionary for fun.

" 'Conformist,' " said Cousin Fred. "Someone who imitates others."

"That's right," said Ferdy. "*I'm* the only really rad cub around. Have you seen anyone else dressed like me lately?"

Trudy smiled sweetly at Ferdy. "I suppose it's just an accident that you dress *exactly* like your uncle Actual Factual," she said. "So who's the conformist?"

"Well,...I...er," said Ferdy. Usually he had a quick answer for everything. But not this time.

"Cool it, you two," said Babs. "We've got better things to talk about than rads and conformists."

"Such as?" said Ferdy.

"Such as why Mr. Grizzmeyer didn't blow his top over Too-Tall's earring," said Babs.

"Isn't it obvious?" said Barry Bruin. "We won, that's all. Mr. G. got tired of fighting us."

"Yeah!" said Lizzy Bruin. "Clear sailing from now on. Seems too good to be true, doesn't it?"

"That reminds me of an old saying," said

Brother Bear. " 'If it seems too good to be true, it probably is.' "

"I'll second that," said Ferdy. "What Brother says shows a great deal of wisdom."

"Oh, you two are just trying to rain on our parade!" said Trudy.

Brother was about to protest. But what happened next saved him the trouble. Queenie McBear dashed into the Burger Bear and hurried to the cubs' booth. She was breathing hard.

"Are you all right?" asked Babs.

"Ran...all the way...from school," gasped Queenie between breaths.

"What's up?" asked Trudy.

"I've got bad news and worse news," said Queenie. "Remember what office Mr. Grizzmeyer came out of this morning?"

The cubs thought for a moment.

"The principal's office?" said Sister.

"Right," said Queenie. "That's the bad news. Mr. Honeycomb has been sent on a month-long tour of Bear Country schools for a university research project. And Mr. Grizzmeyer has been made acting principal!"

"Uh-oh," said Lizzy. The other cubs groaned.

"And what's the worse news?" asked Trudy.

"I know," said Barry. "Mr. G.'s gonna put bars on the windows and change the school's name to Bear Country Prison."

"Worse than that," said Queenie.

"He's going to put up guard towers with machine guns," said Cousin Fred.

"Worse than that," said Queenie.

"He's going to keep us from bringing our lunches to school," said Babs, "so we'll have to eat the school cafeteria food."

"Even worse than that," said Queenie. *"He's putting in a school dress code!"*

A hush fell over the group.

"Can he do that?" asked Barry.

"We'll have no freedom at all!" said Trudy.

"He's not even our real principal!" cried Babs. *"He can't do that!"*

"There's only one problem," said Queenie. "He's already done it. That's why he didn't bother to blow his top at Too-Tall and me this morning. He knew he'd have his dress code all set up in a day or two."

"And that's probably why he was in the office all day," said Trudy. "He was writing the new dress code!"

Queenie pulled a chair up to the booth and sat down. She shook her head sadly and said, "How much would you like to bet the new dress code will be on the main bulletin board when we get to school tomorrow morning?"

Chapter 9
Morning Message

Sure enough, the new dress code was on the school bulletin board the next morning. The cubs gathered around to have a look before classes started.

" 'Bear Country School Dress Code,' " read Babs Bruno out loud. " 'Starting tomorrow, the following rules will be followed by all cubs so that we can have respect, order, and fairness at Bear Country School. 1. No blue jeans with holes in them. 2. No cutoffs. 3. No Batbear capes. 4. No miniskirts...' "

There were about twenty different rules on the list. Not a single type of rad dress was allowed.

"Oh, no!" moaned Trudy Brunowitz. "This is a disaster!"

"Fairness?" said Lizzy Bruin. "Mr. G.'s idea of fairness is to make *everything* against the rules for *everyone*."

"Well," said Ferdy Factual with a smug

smile, "you have to admit—it *is* fair."

"You wouldn't say that if *knickers* were banned!" snapped Trudy.

"Of course I would," said Ferdy. "If a ban on knickers applied to everyone, then it would be fair."

"That shows how much *you* know, smarty," said Trudy. "A ban on knickers would be aimed at one cub—you—because you're the only one who wears them. And that wouldn't be fair. Mr. G. doesn't care about fairness. He just wants to keep us from wearing rad clothes."

Brother Bear kept quiet through all of this. But he was listening carefully. He didn't agree with Ferdy. Most of the time, Mr. Grizzmeyer did care about fairness. But not this time. And respect? It was true that some of the cubs who wore rad clothes didn't respect the teachers. Cubs such as

Too-Tall and the gang. But Too-Tall and the gang could wear three-piece suits to school and they still wouldn't respect the teachers—or anyone else. Most of the cubs who wore rad clothes did respect the teachers and other grownups at school. They even respected Mr. Grizzmeyer.

Brother also believed that most of the rad clothes were so common now that they didn't keep the other cubs from paying attention in class. That was proved by the high test scores in Teacher Bob's class.

As he thought everything over, Brother began to feel more and more on the side of the rads. But since the dress code wouldn't change his own clothing style, he didn't get really angry about it.

That afternoon, though, something happened that finally did get Brother angry about the dress code. *Really* angry.

Chapter 10
The Turning Point

No sooner had Brother and Sister gotten home from school than the doorbell rang. Papa answered it.

"Miss Glitch!" said Papa with surprise. "What can I do for you?"

Miss Glitch stood at the doorstep. A large picnic basket hung on one arm. She reached in and took out a piece of paper and handed it to Papa. "Mr. Grizzmeyer has written a dress code for Bear Country School," she said. "Here is a copy of it."

"Hmm, a dress code," said Papa. "Excellent idea."

"And we've also set up a group called Bears for Order and Respect in Education," said Miss Glitch.

"BORE?" said Papa.

"Yes," said Miss Glitch. "Mr. Grizzmeyer is president, and I'm vice president. We want to help the students understand the dress code and why we need it. We're asking all parents to talk with their cubs about how to dress in order to show respect for others at school."

"I'll do better than that," said Papa. "I'll join up."

"Wonderful!" said Miss Glitch. She reached into her basket again. "Here's a

BORE button for you to wear. And here's a bumper sticker for your car." She held the bumper sticker up for Papa to read. In bold black letters it said: HONK IF YOU'RE A BORE.

"Great," said Papa. "What else can I do to help?"

"Well," said Miss Glitch, "on Monday we're having a special school assembly for BORE speakers. Should I sign you up for that?"

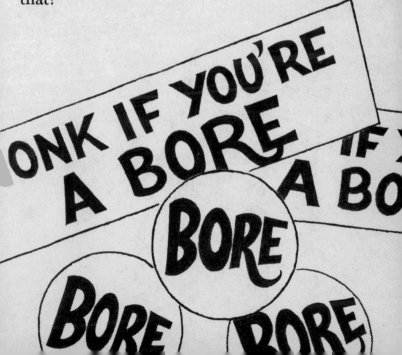

Brother jumped up from the sofa and hurried over. "Hey, wait a minute," he said. "I thought we were having a band concert for assembly on Monday."

"Oh, that's been moved to the following Monday to make room for the BORE program," said Miss Glitch.

"*What?*" said Brother. "Excuse me." He walked back to the sofa and plopped himself down next to Sister. He was furious.

Brother played clarinet in the band. They had been practicing for this concert for weeks. Everyone in the band was eager to get the concert over with and move on to new music.

Something else bothered Brother, too. Mr. Grizzmeyer and Miss Glitch said they were so worried about rad clothes disturbing the day-to-day goings-on at school. But now *they* were disturbing the band concert with their BORE program!

Meanwhile, Papa was saying, "I'd love to speak at the assembly tomorrow, Miss Glitch. I'm against these rad clothes, you know. *My* cubs would *never* wear them."

Miss Glitch frowned and looked past Papa at Sister. She was sure she had seen Sister wearing jeans with kneeholes at school.

Sister noticed Miss Glitch looking at her.

Oh, no! she thought. Don't say anything, Miss Glitch!

Of course, Sister had already changed back into her regular clothes.

Maybe I'm mistaken, thought Miss Glitch. She said good-bye and left.

Whew! thought Sister. That was a close one! She started to roll her eyes at Brother.

But Brother was already upstairs making phone calls to Cousin Fred, Babs, Barry, Lizzy, Ferdy, Trudy, Queenie, and even Too-Tall. To each of them he said the same thing: "Secret meeting at the Burger Bear in half an hour. The usual booth."

Chapter 11
Cat-and-Mouse Game

At the secret meeting at the Burger Bear that afternoon the cubs formed a new group called Freedom and Rights for Each and Every Student. FREES for short. Because it was Brother Bear's idea to form the group, he was made president. Queenie was voted in as vice president. And Babs Bruno, who knew how to tie-dye, was given the job of tie-dyeing FREES on a bunch of T-shirts.

Over the next few days, FREES came up

with a plan to make the new dress code look silly. And on the morning of the BORE assembly, the cubs put the code to the test.

The first cub to be stopped in the hall by Mr. Grizzmeyer was Queenie.

"No jeans with holes," said Mr. Grizzmeyer. "Home you go."

Queenie pointed to the dress code on the bulletin board. "It says no *blue* jeans with holes," she said. "Mine are *green*."

Mr. Grizzmeyer got red in the face. But he let Queenie pass.

Right behind Queenie was Barry Bruin. "Hold it," said Mr. Grizzmeyer. "No cut-offs."

Barry pointed to the frayed edges of his jeans. "I didn't cut them off," he said. "I *ripped* them off."

Mr. Grizzmeyer got even redder. But he let Barry pass, too.

Too-Tall was right behind Barry. Mr. Grizzmeyer held up a hand. "I'm almost afraid to say it," he muttered. "No Batbear capes."

Too-Tall whirled around to show Mr. Grizzmeyer the large red "S" sewn onto the back of his cape. "It's not a Batbear cape, Mr. G.," he said, grinning. "It's a Superbear cape!"

A low growl came from deep down in Mr. Grizzmeyer's throat. But he didn't say a word. Instead, he headed straight for the

office to rewrite the dress code.

That morning's assembly was both good and bad. Even though Brother and Sister loved Papa very much, it really embarrassed them to hear him talk on and on about Respect and Good Manners in front of the whole school. On the other hand, Papa's speech was good publicity for FREES. As soon as it was over, dozens of cubs joined up.

The next morning, Mr. Grizzmeyer tacked a brand-new dress code onto the school bulletin board. And the following morning, he tacked up a whole *new* list of rules. Each time, FREES found new ways of getting around the new rules.

On the fourth day, the cubs gathered around the bulletin board once more to see yet another dress code. But this time there wasn't any list.

Once again, Babs Bruno read the new dress code out loud:

"ANY CUB WEARING CLOTHES THAT MR. GRIZZMEYER THINKS ARE NOT PROPER FOR SCHOOL WILL BE SENT HOME TO CHANGE."

NOTICE
NEW DRESS CODE

The cubs were stunned. They looked at one another in amazement.

"I can't believe it!" said Trudy Brunowitz. "Mr. Grizzmeyer has made himself into a dictator!"

"Nonsense," said Ferdy Factual. "Every principal of Bear Country School has made up some of the rules all by himself. When Mr. Honeycomb comes back, he'll be just as much a dictator as Mr. Grizzmeyer."

"But he won't *act* like one!" snapped Trudy.

"Trudy's right," said Brother Bear. "Sure, Mr. Honeycomb makes up some rules. But he would never keep *changing* the rules just to make things easy for himself. I don't see how we can put up with this."

"What'll we do?" asked Babs.

"We'll go on strike!" cried Queenie. "That's what we'll do!"

"You'd better think that over," said a familiar voice behind the cubs.

They turned and saw the acting principal standing over them with his arms folded across his chest.

"For students," said Mr. Grizzmeyer, "going on strike is the same as playing hooky. And Bear Country has a law against that. You could all get yourselves suspended, even expelled. And your parents could *go to jail.*"

Some of the cubs let out a gasp.

"He's just trying to scare us," Queenie whispered to Brother. "Chief Bruno would never put our parents in jail."

"I heard that!" said Mr. Grizzmeyer. "So, you think I'm bluffing, do you? Well, go ahead. Go on strike. And *see* if I'm bluffing!"

Mr. Grizzmeyer turned and walked calmly down the hall to his office.

The cubs looked shocked. Especially Ferdy Factual. "He's acting like a cub in the schoolyard!" said Ferdy. "He *dared* you to go on strike!"

Of all Brother's and Sister's friends, Ferdy was the only one who had refused to

join FREES. All along he had made fun of the rads. But by now he was really sick of feuding with Trudy. It seemed like such a long time since he'd had a good discussion about mesons and quarks. And now he saw a sure way to get back on Trudy's good side.

The other cubs looked pretty glum. "I don't think Mr. G. is bluffing," said Babs. "We can't strike if it will get our parents in trouble."

"Now hold on," said Ferdy. "Mr. Grizzmeyer may have meant every word he said. But you can still strike."

"How?" asked Cousin Fred.

"Strength in numbers," said Ferdy. "That's what a strike is all about. If you get a whole lot of cubs to strike, there will be too many for Mr. Grizzmeyer to suspend. And there won't be enough jail cells to hold all the parents. Nearly half the cubs at school have already joined FREES. And after the rest see this new dress code, they'll probably all join, too. Let *me* be the first!"

The cubs let out a cheer. "Way to go, Ferdy!" and "Hurray for Ferdy!" they cried.

Brother shook Ferdy's hand and said to

the group, "Strike meeting after school at the Burger Bear!"

The cubs raised their fists in the air and let out another cheer. "Strike! Strike! Strike!" they yelled.

Meanwhile, Trudy ran over to Ferdy and gave him a big hug.

Chapter 12
To Strike or Not to Strike

The week leading up to the big strike was a busy one for both sides. FREES made strike signs and banners and had a march down Main Street. BORE made anti-strike signs and banners and had an anti-strike

march down Main Street. FREES organized a door-to-door campaign to get support for the strike from Bear Country's grownups. And BORE had its own door-to-door campaign to argue against the strike.

Miss Glitch put Papa Bear in charge of the "Door-to-Door for BORE" campaign. He was one of the dress code's biggest supporters. He was sure that the only way to keep the rad clothes from getting stranger and stranger was to outlaw them completely.

Like many other grownups, Mama Bear thought Mr. Grizzmeyer was being too strict. She knew that his and Miss Glitch's hard-nosed rules on rad clothes had only made the cubs dream up more and more unusual fashions. She felt that the dress wars might never have started if Miss Glitch had just warned Queenie about her miniskirt instead of sending her home.

Even so, Mama did not approve of the strike. She didn't want her cubs to miss school because of the dress wars. She hoped some better way of solving the whole problem would come up.

Luckily, just one day before the strike, a better way did come up. Like Mama, Teacher Bob and Teacher Jane did not want to see the school year ruined by a strike. So they suggested that FREES and BORE debate each other in the school auditorium that Saturday. The topic would be "Student Freedom or School Control?"

Mama Bear had a talk with Brother about the debate. She convinced him that Mr. Grizzmeyer might get rid of the dress code if FREES won. And Brother convinced the other members of FREES. So the strike was called off.

There was only one problem. Could the cubs really win the debate?

FREES had another meeting in their favorite booth at the Burger Bear to discuss the debate. They all knew that Ferdy Factual was smart enough to beat the grownups from BORE in a debate, but...

"I'll debate rings around them!" bragged Ferdy. "I'll tie their tongues in knots! I'll make them look like a bunch of

I'LL TIE
THEIR TONGUES
IN KNOTS!

fools...because that's exactly what they are!"

"That's just the trouble," sighed Brother Bear.

"What is?" asked Ferdy.

"You'd probably win on smartness," said Brother. "But you might lose because of *nastiness*."

The other cubs agreed. They thought

hard as they sipped their milk shakes.

Finally, Brother said, "I've got it!"

"What?" asked the others.

"We'll go to Bear Country University and ask Mr. Dweebish for help. He'll know what to do."

Mr. Dweebish was a college professor who had taught social studies at Bear Country School for a while. The cubs all thought he was one of the smartest teachers around. And they knew he would be against Mr. Grizzmeyer's super-strict dress code.

Even Ferdy had to admit that Brother's idea was a good one.

Chapter 13
Dweebish's Secret Plan

FREES decided that its president and vice president should go to the university to meet with Mr. Dweebish. So Brother Bear and Queenie McBear rode the bus to Big Bear City.

In Mr. Dweebish's office, Brother told the professor about their problem.

Mr. Dweebish listened carefully. Then he said, "I've been reading about your dress-code troubles in the *Big Bear City News*. What started it all?"

"Miss Glitch sent me home without a warning and without even checking with Teacher Bob or Mr. Honeycomb," said Queenie. "And I was only wearing something I saw in an old photo of my mom as a cub."

"Hmm," said Mr. Dweebish. "A photo of your mom as a cub...." He leaned back in his chair and gazed thoughtfully out of the window. Suddenly his eyes lit up. The cubs saw them twinkle the way they used to when he taught Foundations of Democracy at Bear Country School.

"What is it?" asked Brother.

Mr. Dweebish put his forearms on the desk and leaned toward the cubs. "I just figured out how I can help you win the debate," he said.

"Great!" said Queenie. "How?"

"I need to make a few phone calls before I let you in on it," said Mr. Dweebish. "Give me your phone number, Brother, so I can get in touch with you."

Brother wrote his number on a piece of notebook paper and handed it to Mr. Dweebish "Call me as soon as you can,"

I JUST FIGURED OUT HOW I CAN HELP YOU WIN THE DEBATE.

Brother said. "The debate is only a few days away, and we need to prepare for it."

"Oh, don't worry about preparing," said Mr. Dweebish with a chuckle. "If my idea works, you'll win the debate without even saying a word."

The cubs looked at each other with raised eyebrows. Win the debate *without even saying a word*? What was Mr. Dweebish talking about?

On the bus home, Brother and Queenie tried to figure out what Mr. Dweebish had in mind. But it was no use.

"It doesn't make sense," said Queenie. "No one can win a debate without saying a word. I think Mr. Dweebish has flipped!"

Brother just shook his head. "I know Mr. Dweebish is smart," he said. "But if he's right about this, he'll be more than smart. He'll be a genius!"

Chapter 14
The Moment of Truth

Saturday came. Bears from all over Bear Country filled the school auditorium for the big debate between FREES and BORE. Many wore T-shirts with FREES tie-dyed on the front. Others wore T-shirts with BORE printed on them.

Cubs and grownups alike were allowed to carry signs into the auditorium. About half the signs said: DEBATE FREES US ALL! The

other half said: BE A BORE LIKE ME!

A slide projector had been set up in front of the stage. Above the podium hung a movie screen. On one side of the podium sat Brother Bear. On the other side sat Papa Bear, Miss Glitch, and Mr. Grizzmeyer.

The audience buzzed as Teacher Bob stepped up to the podium. He called for quiet and asked the audience to lower their signs.

"Ladies and gentlemen, cubs and grownups," he said into the microphone. "Welcome to today's debate between FREES and BORE. The question is: 'Student Freedom or School Control'? FREES has asked to go first, and BORE has agreed. Brother Bear, you may address the audience."

A hush fell over the audience as Brother Bear took Teacher Bob's place at the podium. Everyone was ready for a long speech against the dress code. But Brother did not say a word. Instead, he motioned to Queenie to turn out the lights and signaled to Babs Bruno to start the projector.

A picture came up on the screen. The audience was silent for a moment. Then there were a few giggles. The picture was a photo of Papa Q. Bear as a teenager. He was dressed in a green and purple tie-dyed shirt and red bell-bottom jeans. As the audience looked up at the photo, their giggles turned into laughter.

Brother signaled to Babs again. A new slide came up on the screen. But the laughter in the audience didn't stop. It just got louder.

The slide was a photo of Miss Glitch as a young woman. She was wearing a T-shirt with the words STEEL DRAGONFLY printed

in a circle on it. Inside the circle was a picture of Steel Dragonfly's lead singer, Gor-
geous Grizzly, screaming into a microphone.
The young Miss Glitch also wore a skimpy
little skirt and had daisies tucked behind
her ears.

The third slide drew roars of laughter from the audience. It was a slide of Mr. Grizzmeyer when he was young. He had on a zoot suit with huge pointy shoulder pads and a wide-brimmed hat!

Brother waited for the laughter to get really loud. Only then did he have his helpers shut off the projector and turn on the lights. And as Brother returned to his seat, the audience was still laughing. It seemed as if they would never stop.

Brother spotted Sister, Lizzy, Babs, and Queenie sitting together near the front of the audience. He gave them a big wink. He was so glad they had all been able to keep Mr. Dweebish's plan a secret.

The professor had made the slides from old snapshots given him by Grizzly Gran, Mrs. Grizzmeyer, and Miss Glitch's mother. All three had been happy to help out, because they thought that Mr. Grizzmeyer had gone too far with his dress code.

The laughter continued. Teacher Bob returned to the podium to announce the next speaker. It was BORE's turn to debate.

Teacher Bob looked over at Papa Bear. Papa looked at Miss Glitch. Miss Glitch looked at Mr. Grizzmeyer. None of them budged. Their faces were red with embarrassment.

Finally, Mr. Grizzmeyer motioned for Teacher Bob to come over. He whispered something into his ear.

Teacher Bob went back to the podium and raised his hands for quiet. "BORE has decided not to debate," he announced. "FREES is the winner!"

The audience broke into applause and cheers that seemed to last forever.

Finally, someone from the audience rose and walked to the podium. The moment the audience saw who it was, they stopped applauding and quieted down to listen.

"Thank you for your attention, everyone," said Mr. Honeycomb. "As you can see, I have returned early from my tour of Bear Country schools. I'll be taking over again as principal immediately. One of the many things principals must do from time to time is experiment. Mr. Grizzmeyer has tried a very interesting experiment. But I think it's time for the dress-code experiment to come to an end."

A cheer rang out from all the cubs who had joined FREES. Even some of the grownups applauded.

"Starting Monday," continued Mr. Honeycomb, "there will no longer be a dress code at Bear Country School. And every Friday will be Come-As-You-Are Day for both students *and* teachers."

The debate assembly ended with a standing ovation for Mr. Honeycomb.

Chapter 15
Back to Normal

Mr. Honeycomb's Come-As-You-Are Fridays worked out very well indeed. Cubs began saving their most unusual rad clothes for Fridays. On the other days, they wore more ordinary clothes. Kneeholes got smaller. Cutoffs got longer and neater. Babs Bruno's anklets and toe rings got fewer. Too-Tall forgot all about his capes and stopped wearing his earring. It turned out that he hadn't had his ear pierced after all.

He had just said so to try to get Mr. Grizzmeyer to blow his top.

Sister Bear stopped borrowing Lizzy Bruin's jeans and went back to wearing her usual outfit. But she did buy a pair of jeans with kneeholes to wear on Fridays. And Papa didn't seem to mind! All he said was, "Well, Fridays are Come-As-You-Are Days. Guess you can wear just about anything you want."

One Friday afternoon, Brother and Sister came home from school with scores of 100 on their tests. They proudly handed the tests to Papa and ran off to play. Papa took the tests out to the backyard, where Mama was watering the garden. "Have a look at these," he said. He held up the test papers.

"My goodness!" said Mama. "A pair of perfect scores!"

"And on a Friday, too," said Papa. Then

he looked out into the hazy afternoon sunshine and said, "You know, dear, Mr. Grizzmeyer is a great coach and a terrific gym teacher. But as a principal…well, Mr. Honeycomb seems to run things a lot more smoothly."

Mama just smiled. She had known that all along.